This book belongs to

....

Given by

....

MW00946191

Praise for Mouse Malachi Discovers the Sabbath

"Years ago, I mentioned to a friend that I wished there was a fun way to introduce Christian children to their Jewish roots. Well, here it is! *Mouse Malachi Discovers the Sabbath* is the first in what I hope will be a long line of books designed to teach our precious little ones about that all-important first half of The Book. I've read this in both its rawest form and its edited format, and I'm nearly awash with tears each time. This is a book you will want to have on the bookshelf of your children, your grandchildren, or those children who are dear and special in your life."

—Eva Marie Everson, CEO Word Weavers International, Bestselling Author of *Our God is Bigger Than That!*

"As a pastor and a father, I greatly appreciate Dreama's attention to detail and her ability to teach children in such depth. This book gives each young reader a greater understanding of the Sabbath and will be a staple in our household. Dreama's book captured my attention, as well as the attention of my children as we read together. Her book opens the door for children to ask questions, to grow in their faith, and for families to deepen their understanding of the Sabbath. I highly recommend this book as it serves as a resource needed today."

—Pastor Andy Clapp, Mt. Zion Baptist Church, NC

"The Biblical feasts are so loaded with foreign elements and symbolism that it would seem an impossible topic to write about at a children's level, yet Dreama captures the essence of the feasts and highlights the fine details that would be most meaningful to people of faith. Even though Dreama's poetry is meant for the littles, I believe all age groups can enjoy its treasures.

For those within, Dreama's poetry stirs up warm memories and spiritual convictions. For those who are beginning their journey into learning the feasts, Dreama's words get their toes tapping to the rhythm. As you read this story to your littles, and build their language skills with onset and rhyme, these sweet babies can grow up with an appreciation for learning, diversity, and hunger for more. But don't just stop with the word on the page...there's room at the table for one more and there's freedom to dance in step with Jerusalem's passion."

—Rhonda Perkins, Teacher and Former Leader and Worship Leader in a Jewish Synagogue

Mouse MALACHI discovers the SABBATH

Written by
Dreama Archibald

Illustrated by
Zhi Ling Lee

In Israel we are the mice.
Some people think mice are not nice,
But we must live both us and them,
Together in Jerusalem.

Some mice are dark, and some are light.
Some like the daytime, some like night.
Some mice are dirty, some are clean,
But every mouse must not be seen.

Mouse Malachi is brownish red,
A spot of bright white on his head.
He and his friends have one big home.
They live inside a *catacomb*.

The people dug them long ago,
Like secret hallways deep below,
But in the cracks and all around,
The mice live happy, safe and sound.

While other mice explore the town,
Mouse Malachi just settled down.
He liked his mouse house in the clay,
And never wandered far away.

A friend, Mouse Eva, came to call,
And said, "Let's go explore the hall."
She'd been there many times before,
And knew a secret corridor.

So off she lead him, further in,
Than he had ever, ever been.
But then his eyes could see the light.
They scampered out into the bright.

He followed her into a house,
And was as quiet as a mouse.
The kitchen door was opened wide,
And busy people were inside.

Mouse Eva told him, "It's okay,
Tomorrow is the Sabbath day.
They cook today and clean their best,
Because the Shabbat is for rest."

Just as the sun began to fade,
The work was done, the food was made.
Two candlesticks burned bright and strong,
They sang a special *blessing song*.

Mouse Malachi sat still and watched,
His long black whiskers switched and swatched,
But when they all sat down to eat,
Mouse Malachi jumped to his feet.

"Just settle down," Mouse Eva said.
"The meal will start with juice and bread,
But first, a blessing serenade,
And then a special prayer is prayed."

The father wore a *Ta'lit* shawl,
With fancy corners, strings and all.
The mother wore a pretty veil,
Up on her head with lace detail.

Mouse Eva found a scrap of lace,
And put it on her head, in place.
Around his neck, she put a string.
They skipped around like queen and king.

Then after prayer came juice or wine,
In fancy glasses, tall and fine,
Then crusty bread made in a braid,
Called *challah*, nice and freshly made.

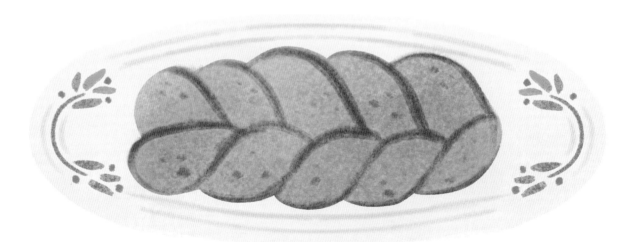

The house was clean, the floors were swept.
After the evening meal, they slept.
They woke up to the sunshine glow,
Then to the synagogue they go.

"*Shabbat Shalom*," the people say,
And that means "Peaceful Sabbath Day."
The greeting sounded oh so nice,
To these excited little mice.

They followed close behind the crowd,
And heard the *Parsha* read aloud.
It's from the *Torah*, people say,
They're books of *Moses* for today.

The mice stretched out under a chair,
And no one knew that they were there,
So then the *Rabbi* came to speak,
The best *derasha* every week.

Mouse Eva hopped up on her feet.
"It's time for everyone to eat.
They call it *oneg*, follow me.
It means *delight*, and I agree."

The crumbs were falling to the ground,
The mice were running all around.
Mouse Malachi had never seen,
Such festive food and fine cuisine.

The *oneg* was a grand delight.
The mice could not eat one more bite.
Their bellies grew and grew and grew.
The mice could barely move—it's true!

The mice knew they must wobble on,
To where the people all had gone.
"They're at the *midrash*," Eva said,
"To talk about the scriptures read."

"They don't just read the *Parsha* though.
Now they're discussing what they know,
And after that it's time for home.
The people say, *Shabbat Shalom*!"

Mouse Eva and Mouse Malachi
Looked at each other with a sigh.
"I guess that we should go home, too.
My daytime nap is overdue!"

So off they hopped along the trails,
With perked up ears and swishing tails.
They made it to the *catacomb*,
Where friend Mouse Eva loved to roam.

They squeaked and talked the whole way down,
The long, dark hallways back to town.
Mouse Eva smiled and waved goodbye,
"*Shabbat Shalom*, Mouse Malachi!"

Glossary
of kid-friendly pronunciations & definitions

Challah /ha-la/ or /chõ-la/
Bread dough made into a braid, baked into yummy bread and eaten on the Jewish Sabbath and Holidays.

Catacomb /cat-u-cōm/
These are tunnels built a really long time ago in ancient times.

Derasha /dē-resh-a/
A proper Jewish name for a sermon or message.

Midrash /mid-rash/
That's when some of the grown-ups get together and talk about the scriptures.

Moses /mō-sis/
The law of God was given to Moses a long time ago.

Oneg /ō-neg/

This means "delight," like Mouse Eva and Mouse Malachi were at the oneg. It's a Sabbath celebration or gathering, in this case, with lots of food!

Parsha /par-sha/

In this story it means a portion, or part of a Jewish scripture being read and talked about.

Rabbi /ra-bī/

A trained Jewish leader who teaches the Jewish scripture.

Shabbat /sha-bot/

This is the Jewish Sabbath. It starts at sundown on Friday and ends at sundown on Saturday.

Shabbatot /sha-bot-ot/

A plural noun, or more than one Shabbat (Jewish Sabbath).

Shabbat Shalom /sha-bot sha-lōm/

When these two words are said together it means, "Have a peaceful day."

Synagogue /si-na-gog/

The place where Jewish people go to worship.

Tallit /ta-lit/ or /ta-lis/

It is a drape or shawl with fringes on the corners that Jewish men wear around their shoulders or over their heads, especially during prayer time. Sometimes women also like to cover their heads during prayer.

Torah /to-rah/

The first five books of the Bible.

About the author, Dreama Archibald

Dreama is an exceedingly blessed NC Southern wife, mom and grandmommy living her best life! She has had a puppet ministry for more than 20 years loving on the senior communities.

Writing stories has been a huge part of Dreama's life for more than 40 years. A rhythm and/or rhyme is the glue she uses to put them together to delight and amuse children as they giggle their way through learning God's truths.

A heartfelt hug and thank you to:

God for salvation and the gift of writing.

My family for their never ending support.

Eva Marie Everson, aka Mouse Malachi, for the inspiration of Mouse Malachi and his adventures.

My daughter, Winter Fixin, for everything technology, and I mean everything and so much more!

Rhonda Perkins, for the wealth of knowledge you so willingly shared.

Serious Writer family and agent, Cyle Young, for pouring into authors and aspiring authors relentlessly.

Mouse Malachi Discovers the Sabbath
Copyright © 2023 by Dreama Archibald / All rights reserved.

No part of this work may be reproduced or transmitted in any form or by any means, electronic or mechanical, including photocopying and recording, or by any information storage or retrieval system, except as may be expressly permitted by the 1976 Copyright Act or in writing from the publisher. Requests for permission can emailed to info@endgamepress.com.

End Game Press books may be purchased in bulk at special discounts for sales promotion, corporate gifts, ministry, fund-raising, or educational purposes. Special editions can also be created to specifications. For details, contact Special Sales Dept., End Game Press, P.O. Box 206, Nesbit, MS 38651 or info@endgamepress.com.

Visit our website at www.endgamepress.com

Library of Congress Control Number: 2022943329
ISBN: 978-1-63797-065-2
eBook ISBN: 978-1-63797-066-9

Published in association with Cyle Young of the Cyle Young Literary Elite, LLC.

Cover & Interior Design by TLC Book Design, TLCBookDesign.com
Illustrated by Zhi Ling Lee with the Bright Agency

Printed in China
10 9 8 7 6 5 4 3 2 1